BEVERLY SILLS
AMERICA'S OWN OPERA STAR

BEVERLY SILLS
AMERICA'S OWN OPERA STAR

BY MONA KERBY
Illustrated by Sheila Hamanaka

VIKING KESTREL

For Deborah Brodie
with warmest appreciation

VIKING KESTREL
Published by the Penguin Group
Viking Penguin, a division of Penguin Books USA Inc.,
40 West 23rd Street, New York, New York 10010, U.S.A.
Penguin Books Ltd, 27 Wrights Lane, London W8 5TZ, England
Penguin Books Australia Ltd, Ringwood, Victoria, Australia
Penguin Books Canada Ltd, 2801 John Street, Markham, Ontario, Canada L3R 1B4
Penguin Books (N.Z.) Ltd, 182–190 Wairau Road, Auckland 10, New Zealand

Penguin Books Ltd, Registered Offices: Harmondsworth, Middlesex, England

First published in 1989 by Viking Penguin, a division of Penguin Books USA Inc.
Published simultaneously in Canada
1 3 5 7 9 10 8 6 4 2
Text copyright © Mona Kerby, 1989
Illustrations copyright © Sheila Hamanaka, 1989
All rights reserved

Women of Our Time® is a registered trademark of Viking Penguin,
a division of Penguin Books USA Inc.

LIBRARY OF CONGRESS CATALOGING-IN-PUBLICATION DATA
Kerby, Mona.   Beverly Sills : America's own opera star / by Mona Kerby ;
illustrated by Sheila Hamanaka.   p. cm.
Summary: Presents a biography of the famous opera singer who
became Director of the New York City Opera.
ISBN 0-670-82251-5
1. Sills, Beverly—Juvenile literature.   2. Singers—United
States—Biography—Juvenile literature.   [1. Sills, Beverly.
2. Singers.]   I. Hamanaka, Sheila, ill.   II. Title.
ML3930.S53K5   1989   782.1'092'4—dc 19   [B]   [92]   89-30225

Printed in the United States of America
Set in Garamond #3

CONTENTS

1

Wait for the Ding Dong!

Bubbles stood before the microphone and looked at the studio audience. She was on the radio. She wasn't afraid. Uncle Bob Emory was standing next to her. Besides, she loved to sing.

And she knew she was good. Last year in Brooklyn, New York, she had been declared Miss Beautiful Baby of 1932.

Now she was four years old. Her blond curls bobbed around her face while she sang her last year's winning talent entry, "The Wedding of Jack and Jill."

The catchy tune ended with the words "ding, dong, ding."

Before she had even come to the end of her song, the audience broke out in applause. "Wait a minute!" she shrieked at them, "I haven't finished my ding dong!"

As the curly-haired baby grew older, she stopped yelling at her audience, of course. But forty years later, her fans were still clapping and cheering for their beloved Bubbles.

Belle Miriam Silverman received her nickname at birth. She was born on May 26, 1929, with an enormous bubble of spit in her mouth. The doctor looked at her and said, "We have to call her Bubbles."

And so they did. In a way, it was a perfect name for her. She was a cute, talkative, funny, bubbly little girl. Her big brothers, Sidney and Stanley, called her Bubbles. Even her parents used the nickname.

She was the third and last child of Morris and Shirley Silverman. Her mother arrived in the United States from Russia when she was fourteen. Her father came to this country from Romania when he was a baby.

During the Depression, when millions of people were out of work and when families went hungry, Morris Silverman worked his way up to become a manager for the Metropolitan Life Insurance Com-

pany. Papa worked hard because he had great plans for his children. They were all going to college, he declared. But Bubbles had plans of her own.

She awoke each morning to the smells of brewing coffee and to the sounds of music. Her mother, Shirley Silverman, started the day by playing Madame Galli Curci records. Galli Curci was a famous Italian soprano during the 1920s. (A soprano is a female singer who sings high notes. A note is a single sound made by a musical instrument or a voice. There are many notes in a song.) Mama had eleven of the singer's records, and she played them over and over again. By the time Bubbles was seven, she had memorized all twenty-two songs. In Italian! (Italian is the language people speak in Italy.)

In the 1930s, when the Depression was the worst, people forgot their troubles at the movies. Shirley Temple, with her bouncing curls and dimpled smile, was the most popular child actress of the time. She danced, sang, and acted in more than 25 films.

Mama believed that all little girls—whether or not they went on to college—should learn how to sing, to tap dance, and to play the piano. So, every Saturday morning, Bubbles went to a downtown school for lessons.

At that school, the star pupils were featured on a local radio show entitled "Uncle Bob's Rainbow

Hour." Bubbles wasn't the best singer or dancer, but she had a large vocabulary, she loved to talk, and she often said something funny. As a result, the four-year-old earned a regular spot on the show.

In the next few years, Bubbles showed off her talents. Once when Uncle Bob rented Town Hall, she sang one of Madame Galli Curci's Italian songs. A New York newspaper reporter teasingly wrote, "That's no seven year old! She's a midget." And, after a talent scout heard her singing the Italian songs in a restaurant, Bubbles got a small part in a movie. Baby Bubbles was a star!

But somehow the name Bubbles Silverman just didn't seem right for a movie star. One of Mama's friends came up with a flashier one. So Bubbles became Beverly Sills.

Bubbles's seventh year was a turning point in yet another way. It was clear to Mama that Bubbles had talent. If her little girl loved to sing, then Mama wanted the very best voice teacher. One day, as they walked down Fifty-seventh Street in New York City, Mrs. Silverman spotted a magazine headline: COACH TO THE WORLD'S GREATEST VOICES. There was a picture of Estelle Liebling. Right then and there, Mrs. Silverman decided to meet the famous teacher.

Miss Liebling thought the lessons were for Mrs. Silverman. Mama explained that they were for Bubbles. "But I don't teach children," Miss Liebling replied. She paused. "In fact, I don't even know any children."

But Miss Liebling agreed to listen. In her most grown-up voice. Beverly began to imitate Madame Galli Curci. Always before, whenever Beverly sang in Italian, adults burst into applause. When she finished this time, however, Miss Liebling burst out laughing. Beverly cried.

Later, Miss Liebling explained that a seven-year-old imitating a world famous opera singer was just plain funny.

Still, Miss Liebling saw that Bubbles was special. Every Saturday morning, she gave Beverly a lesson. Miss Liebling had taught some of the world's greatest opera singers (including Madame Galli Curci!) and her fees were more than the Silvermans could afford. Miss Liebling insisted that the lessons were free.

For 30 years, Miss Liebling was Beverly's one and only voice teacher. "She was more than a teacher to me," Beverly wrote. "She was a second mother."

Miss Liebling worked with her young and talented student. And when that student grew up, the name Beverly Sills would become one of the most famous names in the world.

2

Elephants
in the Mail

Ten-year-old Beverly sat beside Mama in the opera theater. She was excited. Slowly the lights dimmed. She watched as the conductor walked toward the orchestra and bowed to the audience. He turned and lifted his hands. Music filled the air. The curtain rose. Actors and actresses in lovely costumes began to sing. The story was told by the music.

When it was over, Beverly jumped to her feet and shouted "Bravo!" for the men opera stars. For the women opera stars, she shouted "Brava!"

By the age of ten, Beverly knew what she wanted

to be—an opera star, "not an opera singer, but a star."

Beverly knew that singing an opera was very hard work. First of all, the opera singer must have a wonderful voice and must have years of musical training. The singer must be able to sing in English, Italian, French, and German because operas are written in many languages. Also, an opera singer must be able to act and to dance.

With Miss Liebling as a teacher, Beverly began to train. She took piano lessons. She took French and Italian lessons. She read operas that were written in those languages and then rewrote them in English.

On Saturdays, Beverly had her singing lessons. From Brooklyn, it was a four-hour round-trip to Miss Liebling's studio. To get there, Mama and Beverly had to take a bus, a trolley, and two subways. When Beverly grew older, she made the trip alone with money pinned inside her bloomers.

On Sundays, she performed on the radio. Beverly won a contest and became a regular member of "Major Bowes Capitol Family Hour." This program was heard by millions of people all over the United States.

Once when Major Bowes stated that Beverly was holding a small glass elephant for luck, she received hundreds more in the mail. Another time, Beverly wished that she might have a sled since it was snowing. Twenty-two listeners sent sleds. (She was allowed to

keep one; the rest were sent to orphans.) "From then on," Beverly said later, "anytime I wanted anything I just mentioned it over the air."

Beverly performed in other shows. For 36 weeks, she acted and sang in a soap opera called "Our Gal Sunday." She sang a commercial for soap and made it famous: "Rinso White, Rinso White, happy little wash day song." She was even on a TV program called "Stars of the Future."

Miss Liebling invited Beverly and Mrs. Silverman to dinner parties with famous singers. After dinner, Beverly would sing for the guests. And because Miss Liebling gave them tickets, Mama and Beverly often went to the opera.

Beverly had many lessons and spent much of her time with adults. Years later, her brother Stanley said that Beverly "never had a childhood."

Although Beverly was busy, sometimes she did things just for fun. She went to the movies. She loved to read. And she went with her brothers to Ebbetts Field to watch the Brooklyn Dodgers play baseball. But even then her dream was not forgotten. Her brothers would tell her, "Stop shouting, Bubbly. You'll hurt your voice."

One of Beverly's favorite things to do was to talk. Papa was always telling her, "Lower your voice, cutie, lower your voice. It bothers me."

Beverly's high voice was perfect for singing soprano. But because Beverly loved to talk so much, she learned to speak in a low voice. When she grew up, people were always surprised that her speaking voice was low and her singing voice was high.

Papa Silverman did not want his little girl to be in show business. He wanted his children to be educated. When Beverly was 12, she stopped performing. Papa wanted her to, and she agreed. Beverly continued her singing lessons, but now more than anything, she just wanted to be a teenager.

She was an editor of her school newspaper. She chatted for hours with her friends. She had a boyfriend. He used to whistle her Rinso White commercial whenever he wanted her to come outside. Papa would ask her, "Are you going out with a boy or a bird?"

In 1942, Beverly graduated from P.S. 91. She made her graduation dress. It was the first and last dress she ever made. She was voted Prettiest Girl, Most Likely to Succeed, Fashion Plate, Most Talented, and Most Personality.

While Beverly was in school, the Silvermans lived in Brooklyn. Their house was typical—three rooms on the first floor and three bedrooms upstairs. Beverly helped with the "victory garden" in the backyard.

During World War II, Americans and their allies

fought Germany and Japan. U.S. children helped with gardens as a way of saving food for the soldiers. Both of Beverly's brothers were soldiers. By working in the garden, Beverly felt she was helping them win the war.

After Beverly graduated from the eighth grade, she entered Erasmus High School. But by the time she was fifteen, she was tired of being just a teenager. She was ready to perform again.

Mama and Papa and Beverly spent hours talking about Beverly's future. In almost every discussion, Papa had the last word.

Once Papa told Beverly not to smoke or to drink. He didn't give her a choice. So Beverly didn't. That was that.

But Beverly's career was an entirely different matter. She had to make Papa understand. During supper one evening, Beverly pleaded with her mother to explain it all to her father. "Listen, Morris," Mama said, "the child wants to be an opera star." Papa never looked up from his soup. "The child will go to college and be smart."

And then Mrs. Silverman did something unusual. She talked back to her husband. "No, Morris, the two boys will go to college and be smart. *This* one will be an opera singer."

The argument was dropped for the evening. Beverly knew twenty operas already, but even if Papa had said yes, she was still too young to get a job with an opera company.

But Beverly wasn't too young to sing in an operetta. An operetta is an opera which is sung in English and is often funny. Beverly—with her high soprano voice, her bubbly personality, and her acting ability—was perfect for singing comedies. J.J. Schubert was hiring singers to travel from town to town, performing operettas. He offered Beverly Sills a job.

Papa said no. Beverly was too young to travel around the country by herself, and he needed Mama at home. Finally, Mama and Beverly convinced Papa to let his little girl go. Mama arranged for one of the older girls in the cast to be Beverly's chaperone. (A chaperone is usually an older, married woman who watches over a younger girl in public.) Once, Beverly's chaperone used a homemade recipe on Beverly's hair to keep it blond. When the chaperone measured the ingredients incorrectly, Beverly's hair came out red. Beverly liked it. She's been a redhead ever since!

In 1945, the sixteen-year-old was traveling with J.J. Schubert's company and was making $100 a week. Since she was traveling, she couldn't attend classes. She enrolled in the Professional Children's School in Manhattan. They allowed her to skip classes and mail in her homework.

Papa did not like this kind of school for his daughter. When she turned down a math scholarship to college, Papa was even sadder. He was afraid that Beverly was not paying enough attention to her studies.

Soon after that, Beverly's chaperone began spending too much time with her boyfriends. She was replaced by another. The new chaperone later was convicted of murder.

Both Mama and Papa insisted that Beverly quit and return home. With no grown-up to take care of her, they worried about her safety. She was gone three months at a time. Besides, she was neglecting her voice lessons, and she wasn't learning new operas.

Beverly was given a choice—either return to her music lessons or go to college to become a teacher. J.J. Schubert agreed with her parents. Show business, he said, would not help her if she was serious about an opera career.

Beverly chose voice lessons. Every day for the next few years, she practiced singing and learning new operas. Her lessons took so much time that she didn't perform very often.

In 1949, when Beverly was twenty, she was asked to sing on a three-week cruise ship bound for South America. Beverly had a wonderful time. When she returned home, Mama met her at the ship dressed in black. Papa was dead.

Beverly was shocked. She knew Papa had lung cancer—she and Mama had moved to a small apartment near his hospital. But Beverly had been so excited about the cruise, she didn't fully understand that Papa was dying. And because her parents did not want to spoil her fun, they didn't tell her the truth.

Papa and Beverly had disagreed on the best career for her. Still, he loved and helped her. Now he would never get to see her dreams come true.

3

Stinking Smut

One morning, on the way back from a voice lesson, Beverly window-shopped. She must have been humming because a man asked if she was a singer and offered her work. A private club for the very rich needed a singer from ten at night until three in the morning. Even though the hours were terrible and her mother wasn't pleased, Beverly took the job. She sang popular songs as well as songs from opera. Within two years, Beverly had saved enough money for a trip to Europe.

Summer in Paris was wonderful. She and Mama

stayed at a small hotel. With Miss Liebling's help, Beverly was accepted into the Paris Opera Acting School. There were eight singers; Beverly was the only American. She added more songs to her French repertoire. (A repertoire, "REP-er-twar", is a list of songs that a singer can perform.) Her French also improved.

Twenty-two-year-old Beverly returned to New York in the fall of 1951, eager to sing opera. Once again, Miss Liebling helped her. She arranged for Beverly to audition, to try out, with the great opera director, Charles Wagner. He had organized an opera touring company, the only one of its kind. After he heard Beverly sing, he told her, "Miss Sills, you are going to be a star."

So Beverly was on the road again, but this time she was singing opera. Money was tight. Mama made all of her clothes as well as all of her costumes.

Touring was by bus and by truck. The truck carried the equipment—musical instruments, costumes, stage scenery. The bus carried the musicians. They traveled as much as 350 miles a day to get to the next stop, which was often a high school auditorium in a small town. They performed 63 nights in a row. To pass the time on the bus, Beverly read, dozed, or played cards. They slept in cheap hotels and ate in cheap restaurants.

Local newspapers often praised Beverly's singing. "My voice was all right," Beverly said, "but my feet were killing me."

One time, the bus pulled into a small town in Nebraska where the cattle were sick with a disease called "stinking smut." On the day of the concert, Beverly's picture was in the newspaper and was called "Stinking Smut." Under a picture of a dead cow it said "Beverly Sills."

The tours were good experience. Now Beverly had performed more than 100 times. Even so, in 1953, she was out of work again.

Whenever Beverly was asked to sing opera, she said yes. But the work wasn't regular. Since 1952, she had tried out seven times for Dr. Joseph Rosenstock, the director at the New York City Opera. Each time she was turned down.

In 1955, her agent wanted her to audition again. But Beverly didn't really want to. She asked her agent to find out what was the matter. Dr. Rosenstock said that Beverly had a great voice, but she didn't have any personality.

Beverly was angry. She was very angry. How dare he say that Bubbles, formerly Miss Beautiful Baby of 1932, didn't have any personality. She'd show him a thing or two.

On the day of the audition, Beverly sang two arias

(AR-ee-uhs), or songs, that weren't even right for her high voice. She glared at Dr. Rosenstock. And for some strange reason, Dr. Rosenstock smiled. Maybe he thought opera singers were supposed to be difficult. Rosenstock gave Beverly a job with the New York City Opera.

At last! Beverly had a permanent job at one company. This meant that during every opera season, she would have some role to sing. She still wasn't a star, but at least she was an honest-to-goodness opera singer. Pretty good for stinking smut!

4

52 Round-Trip Tickets

In her wildest dreams, Beverly never expected a wink, a matchbook, and a smoky fireplace would lead to her marriage. But in a way, that's what happened.

In November 1955, the New York City Opera performed in Cleveland, Ohio. After the Friday night opera, there was a party. All evening, a big handsome blond-haired man kept winking at Beverly. He even gave her a matchbook with his phone number scribbled inside.

On Saturday night, there was another opera party. Again the big handsome man winked at Beverly. He asked Beverly to have supper with him on Sunday, but she said no. She explained that she was flying home after the last performance of the opera. On Sunday, Beverly changed her mind. She dialed the number on the matchbook.

The man and two little girls picked up Beverly at the hotel. "Are you going to be our new mommy?" one of them asked.

Beverly began to worry.

They ate dinner at the man's new home. The 25 room mansion stood on the shores of a lake. After dinner, the man started a fire in the fireplace. Smoke filled the room.

Tears came to Beverly's eyes. Coughing, she crept to the kitchen. There at the kitchen table, Beverly and the big handsome man talked. And that's when Beverly knew that she was in love with Peter Greenough (say it "GREEN-no").

Peter Greenough was from a very old Boston family. One of his relatives, John Alden, arrived in America on the Mayflower in 1620. Peter's family owned the local newspaper in Cleveland.

Peter was the father of three daughters. One was mentally retarded and living in a special hospital. He was in the middle of a divorce. He was thirteen years older than Beverly.

When Beverly arrived home the next day, she explained everything to her mother. "Mama, I think I've met a man I could marry!"

Mama burst out crying.

In time, Mrs. Silverman learned to like Peter. For one thing, he was very thoughtful. Mama went with them on all of their dates. (She didn't want Beverly to be seen alone with a married man.) Peter brought Mama flowers and paid attention to her. Also, Peter was sometimes very bossy. Papa had been both thoughtful and bossy. Beverly and Mrs. Silverman loved Peter because he was a lot like Papa.

Now Beverly's life revolved around singing and Peter. That year, she had parts in three different operas. In October, when Peter's divorce was final, he gave her a diamond ring.

They were married in Miss Liebling's studio on November 17, 1956. And bubbly Beverly, who loved to talk, had a terrible sore throat. During their honeymoon, Beverly couldn't say a word to her new husband.

The first year of their marriage was very hard. Beverly loved Peter, but the large home, the servants, and her new stepdaughters were a big responsibility.

Also, their different religions caused problems for their family and friends. Some of them wouldn't speak to Beverly because she was Jewish. Others wouldn't speak to Peter because he was Christian. This hurt their

feelings. Beverly was lonely. She hated Cleveland. She traveled for months at a time, singing in different places.

Beverly had a job with the New York City Opera, but she did not go to work every day. The City Opera's fall season lasted less than two months. Beverly would sing in two different operas for a total of five or six nights. Of course, before she performed, she spent time learning her part, taking voice lessons, and rehearsing with the other musicians.

For the rest of the year, Beverly sang wherever she was asked—Texas, Florida, New York, Massachusetts, Tennessee, Illinois, and Ohio. Peter joined her as often as he could.

Even though Beverly was being invited to sing in different places, she was not well-known. Once, during a snowstorm, she performed in a school auditorium. There were only thirty people in the audience.

In the spring of 1958, for the first time ever, the New York City Opera was presenting American operas. This was unusual because most operas are sung in other languages. The City Opera was having money trouble, and they were trying to get people to come to the opera. Julius Rudel, who by now was the director of the company, held auditions for "The Ballad of Baby Doe."

The Ballad of Baby Doe was set in Colorado and was

based on a true love story. A man named Horace Tabor made a fortune in the silver mines. He left his wife for Baby Doe, the wife of a miner. Tabor went bankrupt and died in Baby Doe's arms. Before he died, he asked her never to sell "the Matchless Mine." Later, Baby Doe froze to death at the entrance of the mine.

Beverly wanted the role. The music was perfect for her high coloratura ("kuh-ler-uh-TYOO-ruh") voice. Coloratura singers sing many different notes very fast. They often trill, or rapidly sing two notes over and over again.

But she did not audition. Beverly had heard that the composer was looking for a small woman and she was sensitive about being tall and large-boned. Rudel insisted that she try out.

Once again, Beverly Sills marched on stage in a fit of anger. The 5'8" Bubbles wore high heeled shoes and a tall cap. She stood well over six feet.

Beverly looked down at Mr. Moore, the composer. She dared him to say she was too tall to play Baby Doe. Instead, the surprised man listened to Beverly sing. After she finished, he said, "Miss Sills, you are Baby Doe."

The Ballad of Baby Doe was a smash hit. Of all the roles that Beverly sang in her career, she always felt that Baby was one of her very best.

These were good years for Beverly. Music experts often wrote about her in newspapers and praised the way she sang. One event, however, was more important to Beverly than singing or praise. On August 4, 1959, she gave birth to their daughter, Meredith. They called her Muffy.

Beverly loved being a mother. She stopped performing at the New York City Opera and devoted herself to Peter and their daughters. They moved to Boston where Peter wrote for one of the newspapers. Sometimes Beverly peformed in other cities, but mostly she stayed at home with her family.

On June 29, 1961, Peter Greenough Jr. was born. "Bucky" was the first male child born to the Green-

ough family in 47 years. Beverly and Peter were even happier.

One day, when Muffy was nearly two, she started to touch the stove. Beverly yelled at her. "Hot! Hot! Hot!" Muffy smiled and repeated "hot." It was the first word she had ever spoken. It probably was the first word Muffy had ever heard.

Although Beverly had wondered why her little girl did not talk, the doctors had said that everything was fine. Soon after this, however, the Greenoughs had Muffy's hearing testing. They discovered that Muffy was deaf.

Six weeks later, they discovered that Bucky was

retarded. Their first clue was when a baby photographer tried to get Bucky's attention. "Hey, lady," the man said, "There's something wrong with your son. I can't get him to look at the birdie."

One doctor told the Greenoughs, "There are so many things wrong with this boy that if I listed them today, they would be only half of what you're going to be facing."

Bucky lay for hours without moving. He did not look at people. He did not speak. When he was five, he had his first epileptic seizure. His whole body jerked. To keep him from swallowing his tongue, his parents put a spoon in his mouth and turned him on his side. Bucky's problems had so many problems that he was 22 years old before they discovered he was also deaf.

After Beverly learned that Bucky was retarded, she went into shock. She did not leave the house. She stopped flying to New York for her weekly voice lesson.

Beverly felt sorry for herself. It just wasn't fair. Why did she have to suffer more than other people?

Mama, Peter, her brothers and her friends were worried about Beverly. Julius Rudel began writing funny letters addressed to "Dear Bubbela" from "Julius Darlink." He wanted her to come back to work. She told Julius that she couldn't sing anymore.

Finally, Julius insisted that she return to the opera company. After all, she had signed a contract promising to sing.

In 1962, for her thirty-third birthday, Peter gave her 52 round-trip tickets from Boston to New York. It was the best present Beverly could have received.

5

Cleopatra or Quit

Beverly still felt sorry for herself and for her children. She once said, "There's never a moment that I'm not aware that something's wrong. You really cannot brush it off; it's a kind of hopelessness that sits on you forever."

But Beverly did learn to cope. Her family helped her. Peter invented Adult Day. The two of them went to the theater and ate at nice restaurants. Mama reminded her that Muffy was perfectly normal in every way but one; she just couldn't hear. As for Bucky, Mama told Beverly to be thankful that she could afford the very best care for him. Even Muffy helped Beverly. She spent hours learning how to speak, yet she never complained. She just kept trying.

So Beverly followed her daughter's example. She didn't complain. Whenever she was around people, she acted cheeful and happy. She laughed a lot. Beverly explained, "My inner . . . feelings were nobody's business but my own."

With her 52 round-trip tickets, Beverly started flying to New York for her weekly voice lessons. She began to perform in operas. And she discovered something wonderful.

Ever since Beverly was a little girl, she had loved to sing. But now she liked singing for a new reason. Whenever she walked on stage, dressed in her costume, she became the person she was playing. During the opera, Beverly completely forgot her troubles. Opera was an escape from her sadness. She sang for pure pleasure. Audiences sensed her joy and were enchanted.

As a result, Beverly was asked to sing more often. She sang for the New York City Opera, the New Orleans Opera, and for the Boston Opera. In Boston, Beverly became close friends with Sarah Caldwell, who is one of the few women opera directors and conductors in the world.

Between 1962 and 1965, Beverly starred in many

operas. In *The Tales of Hoffman,* she played three characters, one of whom was Olympia, a mechanical singing doll. Beverly wore huge eyelashes and big red circles pasted on her cheeks. In *The Magic Flute,* Beverly played a magical queen. In *Faust,* she played Marguerite who falls in love with the devil, kills her son, goes to prison, prays to God, dies, and goes to heaven. Even though all of the operas were different, Beverly was good in every role.

Beverly Sills was becoming well-known among opera singers and directors. They nicknamed her "Iron Lung" because she sang when she was ill and because she could sing while lying down. Beverly could learn a new part in a few days. And, she would substitute for another singer with only a few hours' notice.

But above all, Beverly was known for her wonderful voice. Winthrop Sargeant, the music critic for *The New Yorker,* had begun calling Beverly the prima donna of the New York City Opera. A prima donna is the most important woman singer in an opera company.

In New York City, there are two opera houses. Beverly sang for the smaller, local one. Many local opera companies have to struggle to get enough money to pay for singers, musicians, stage sets, costumes, and rent on the building.

Because everything was so expensive, the New York City Opera sometimes had a short season. This meant that they might have three or four operas in a two-month period and then close for the rest of the year.

The other opera company in New York City is the Metropolitan. People think of the Met as the opera company for the entire United States. It's one of the greatest opera companies in the world. Only the most famous opera stars are invited to sing at the Met. The Met spends hundreds of thousands of dollars for each opera production. There aren't many cities that are large enough to have two opera companies. Perhaps that is why they compete and there are sometimes problems between the two.

In 1966, the New York City Opera and the Metropolitan both moved into new homes. The city opera and the ballet company shared the New York State Theater. The Met moved into a larger, more elegant theater, which they didn't have to share. Now the opera companies were even closer. Both theaters were in the new Lincoln Center, right next to each other.

For some reason, both companies planned similar operas for their opening nights in the fall of 1966. The Met scheduled Samuel Barber's *Antony and Cleopatra* while the City Opera scheduled Handel's *Julius*

Caesar. Cleopatra was an Egyptian queen of long ago who fell in love with two Roman rulers, Caesar and Antony.

At the City Opera, Julius Rudel assigned the part of Cleopatra in "Julius Caesar" to Phyllis Curtain, one of their former singers who was now under contract with the Met. Because Phyllis sang for the Met, she was more famous than Beverly. Julius wanted a big name for opening night. When Beverly heard the news, she was not bubbly.

Beverly talked and pleaded with Julius. He didn't change his mind. Finally, she lost her temper. "If I don't get Cleopatra," she yelled, "I quit!"

Beverly added that if she wasn't chosen, her rich husband was going to rent Carnegie Hall and Beverly would sing every one of Cleopatra's arias, or songs. To top it off, Beverly hired a publicity agent who made certain her name made the news. Nobody was going to tell her that she wasn't good enough or famous enough to sing.

Julius Rudel changed his mind. Beverly said that there were no hard feelings. He and Phyllis Curtain remained her good friends.

Beverly began training every day. She hired a new teacher, Roland Gagnon, who was much younger than Miss Liebling. Roland taught Beverly different ways to sing. Beverly believed that Roland could teach her

better than Miss Liebling. Beverly loved Miss Liebling and she knew that her feelings were hurt. But more than anything else, Beverly wanted to be good on opening night.

From the very beginning of rehearsals, Beverly surprised everyone. Even Julius, who had worked with her for years, asked her where she had learned to sing that way. "But Julius," Beverly replied, "I've always sung this way. It's just that nobody has ever heard me."

For the first time, Beverly could show off her talents. The Cleopatra arias were difficult, yet Beverly sang the high notes rapidly and easily. One aria had to be sung very high and very fast. It lasted six minutes and Beverly had to look as if she wasn't breathing.

As soon as Beverly walked on stage, people couldn't help but watch her. She was also a wonderful actress.

From around the world, music critics, opera directors, and opera lovers came to New York for the grand opening at the Metropolitan Opera. They were all disappointed. The expensive production of *Antony and Cleopatra* was a flop. One critic even called the production a "shipwreck."

Since the critics were already in New York and since the New York City Opera was just a few steps away, they decided to attend the opening of *Julius Caesar.*

That night something special happened at the City Opera. The entire cast was terrific. Whenever Beverly sang, the audience sat on the edge of their seats. At the end, they roared with delight. Beverly wrote, "I knew that I had sung as I have never sung before."

The critics went wild with praise. One wrote, "If I were recommending the wonders of New York to a tourist, I should place Beverly Sills way ahead of such things as the Statue of Liberty and the Empire State Building."

At long last, Beverly Sills was a star.

6

Eating Peanut
Clusters

And what did Beverly have to say for all this attention?
Maybe it came too late in life for her to be truly
impressed. After all, she didn't become famous until
she was in her late thirties. She said, "I went through
so many years when nobody wanted me. . . . Suddenly
I'm the Beatles of opera." (The Beatles were the most
popular rock group in music history.)

After her performance in *Julius Ceasar*, she was
invited to sing all over the world. Beverly traveled
everywhere, singing nearly anything. Within one
three-week period, she sang on three different con-

tinents—North America, South America, and Europe. Beverly wrote, "Queens, madwomen, country girls, army mascot, I sing 'em all."

Beverly was once asked how she stayed so happy. "I'm not always happy," she replied, "but I always try to be cheerful." She added, "If I feel a self-pity urge coming on, know what I do? Eat a peanut cluster and get on with life."

She really tried to keep her sadness private, but sometimes this was hard to do. In 1967, when Bucky was six, Beverly and Peter had to place him in a special hospital. He had never learned to take care of his own needs.

On the day they took Bucky to live in the special hospital, Beverly sang *Il Trittico,* three of Puccini's one-act operas. In one of them, Beverly portrayed a mother who abandoned her son. While Beverly sang her role, she cried. Later the director said, "It was the only hysterical performance I have ever seen her give." Beverly never sang the part again.

In October 1969, Beverly played a madwoman in *Lucia de Lammermoor.* At the conclusion, the audience clapped for seven minutes. Beverly had performed with a 103° temperature. The *Time* magazine music critic wrote that Beverly was one of "the most spectacular singers in the world."

Why did people think Beverly was a spectacular

singer? Certainly one reason was the way she showed her love of singing. Another reason was her skill as an actress. But the most important reason was her voice. One conductor said, "The unique thing about Beverly's voice is that she can move it faster than anybody else alive."

In the spring of 1969, Beverly received an offer to sing in Italy, at one of the world's most famous opera houses, La Scala. Rossini's *The Siege of Corinth* had not been performed at La Scala in over 100 years. Beverly would star as Palmira.

Soon after Beverly arrived in Italy, she lost her patience during a rehearsal. One of the costumes was made of gold fabric, but Beverly and the designer agreed that it should be made in silver. Several times Beverly reminded the seamstress, and the woman always told Beverly not to worry. At the final fitting, the dress was still gold. Beverly walked on stage, folded the dress and cut it up. The seamstress was very angry, but the Italian opera singers and stage hands cheered and clapped.

On opening night, they applauded again. Beverly's performance was magnificent. She managed to sing six notes to the count of one. She even sang 32nd notes. (Try counting slowly—one number to a second. In the time it takes you to say one number, Beverly could sing six notes. By the time you get to

four, Beverly could sing 32 notes.) The Italian audience loved her. They nicknamed her "La Sills" and La Fenomena" (the phenomenon). Beverly liked the nickname "Il Mostro". Not only did it mean "the incomparable" but also it meant "the monster".

That week, her picture made the cover of *Newsweek* magazine. Wherever she went, people knew who she was.

In 1970, Beverly tackled a difficult project. Donizetti, an Italian who lived in the 1800s had written three operas which focused on the lives of three English queens. No modern soprano had ever sung all three roles. Beverly Sills decided she would be the first.

Miss Liebling was against it. She said that the roles were too demanding. They would hurt her voice. But Beverly's mind was made up. Every day for months, she practiced her singing with Roland Gagnon.

In October 1970, at the New York City Opera, Beverly played Queen Elizabeth I in *Roberto Deveraux*. In this opera, Queen Elizabeth is an old woman. It took two hours to apply Beverly's makeup. Her dress, designed to make Beverly look old, weighed 55 pounds. For three hours every night, Beverly wore it while she moved around the stage and sang. On some nights, Beverly lost as much as 8 pounds.

At the end of Act II on opening night, the crowd

stood up, clapped and yelled. "Brava! Brava!" This was Beverly's first standing ovation during the middle of an opera.

In March 1972, she starred as the second English queen, *Maria Stuarda*. And in 1973, she completed the third role in *Anna Bolena*. (During that performance, she lost two caps off her teeth. She managed to pick them up and stick them back in her mouth.)

Beverly received many honors. She was appointed to the National Endowment for the Arts. She was named the March of Dimes' National Chairman of the Mother's March on Birth Defects. She was also invited to sing for President Richard Nixon at the White House. On that evening, her zipper broke. She backed up, grabbed her coat, and kept on singing.

Beverly traveled as much as 250,000 miles in a year. In January 1974, she visited ten U.S. cities, performing for sold-out audiences. Beverly was one of the highest paid opera singers in the world, with an average salary of $400,000 a year. Because Peter was so rich, Beverly's family never lived on her salary. Instead, she saved her money for her children.

For much of 1974, Beverly was in a great deal of pain. That fall, when Beverly was in Dallas rehearsing for a new role, her brother, Sidney, a doctor, called. He ordered her back home to have an operation for cancer. Within three weeks, she was performing in

San Francisco and Los Angeles. "I just didn't want people to think I was dead!" she said.

Beverly handled the highs and lows of her career by following her mother's advice: "Find a thought that will make you cheerful and forget the sad thoughts. Think pink."

Beverly Sills' name and picture was splashed across every major newspaper and magazine in the United States. Writers loved to interview her. She told great stories and she laughed a lot.

Beverly also appeared on national television. Once on "The Tonight Show," she and Johnny Carson performed together. They sang "Indian Love Call," a famous song from an old movie. Johnny Carson was so funny that Beverly burst out laughing. On Thanksgiving Day in 1976, Americans watched "The Carol Burnett Show." Carol and Beverly sang and danced together. In one scene, Carol and Beverly dressed up like dolls and sucked their thumbs. In another scene, they wore top hats and did the high kick.

And Americans enjoyed Beverly's performance in *The Merry Widow*. This was one of the first operas ever to be televised live. In this light-hearted comedy, a man confuses his wife with another woman. Beverly played the other woman.

Even children watched Beverly. On one Muppet TV special, she sang with some of Miss Piggy's pals.

Beverly combined talent, personality, and publicity. She made opera popular. Before, most Americans thought opera was for Europeans or for rich people. But after Americans saw Beverly on TV and read about her in the newspapers, thousands of people began to buy opera tickets and opera records.

Life seemed better than Beverly had ever expected. She had fame and fortune. She had a family who loved her. Bucky was receiving good care. Muffy was growing into a lovely young woman. Even though she was deaf, she was learning to speak. Still, Beverly had one dream that had never come true.

She had sung at every major opera house in the world, except for one. Beverly Sills had never been invited to sing at the Metropolitan Opera, America's grandest opera house.

The Met was run by Sir Rudolph Bing from 1950 to 1972. Mr. Bing had hired only a few New York City Opera singers. He believed that American singers were not as good as European singers.

Mr. Bing invited Beverly to sing on dates when he knew that she was already busy. He had given her just one chance to sing for the Met. She sang in an outdoor concert of *Don Giovanni*. To Beverly's way of thinking, a baseball park was not the same as an elegant opera house.

Beverly never knew why Mr. Bing did not like her.

Perhaps it was because she was an American. But one thing was perfectly clear. Mr. Bing did not want Beverly to sing at the Met.

After many years, Mr. Bing retired. And within a few months, the new head of the Met, Goeran Gentele, had scheduled a date for Beverly to sing. Finally, on April 8, 1975, Beverly Sills starred at the Metropolitan Opera—twenty years after her debut (day-BYOO") or first performance, at the New York City Opera and six years after her debut at La Scala. She was 45 years old.

That spring, the tension was enormous. Beverly easily could have failed. After all, most singers' voices have faded by middle age. She was still recovering from surgery. News reporters wrote about her. Everyone wondered if Beverly would be good.

She starred in the same opera in which she had performed at La Scala and one that had never been presented at the Met—*The Siege of Corinth*. The cheapest tickets sold for $60 and the most expensive sold for $500. Still, all five performances were sold out, and 7,000 people had to be turned away.

At 8:00 P.M., the conductor began the opera. At 8:22, Beverly walked on stage, wearing a long blue gown.

She never had a chance to sing her opening line, "What do I hear?" One critic wrote: "She knew what she heard—a minute long roar of welcome. . . . At evening's end, the curtain calls went on for 18½ minutes. Out in the audience, opera-loving comedian Danny Kaye let out several ear-piercing whistles and called for a speech. Confetti and roses floated down from the upper tiers, several bouquets came sailing across the orchestra pit."

As a little girl, Beverly had dreamed of this very moment. So what did she do? She cried!

7

"I've Done That Already"

From 1975 until 1980, Beverly earned about seven and a half million dollars. While she hated to give up the money, she was more than ready to retire. As an opera star, Beverly had accomplished her goals. Besides, she and Peter had a saying—"I've done that already."

On October 27, 1980, at the age of 51, Beverly Sills sang for the very last time.

Her final performance was held at the New York City Opera. Beverly insisted that the evening be a celebration. They decided to produce the second act of *Die Fledermaus*. The setting was a New Year's Eve Ball with a variety of entertainers. That night, the New York City Opera was packed. Many of the guests paid $1,000 each for their tickets. Famous stars walked on stage and dazzled the audience with their talents.

At the evening's end, Beverly praised her teacher, Estelle Liebling (who had died ten years earlier). Then she sang a farewell song. The audience cheered and applauded. Beverly walked offstage. When the audience continued to cheer, she returned once more. Confetti and balloons filled the house. With one last bow, Beverly Sills's singing career was over.

The next morning, she started work as the General Director of the New York City Opera. She has never sung again. Her voice deserved a rest, she said. "I won't even hum in the shower."

As General Director, Beverly took charge of money and the production of operas. From the very beginning, emotions were tense in the basement offices of the City Opera. Beverly replaced her long time friend, Julius Rudel, who was forced to quit. Julius once explained that he knew music, but he didn't know much about money and how to manage the opera's business. Their friendship suffered. The office staff resented Beverly for taking over after Julius.

After years of being praised, Beverly was now

widely criticized. Singers weren't smart enough to run a business, people told her. What's more, they added, a woman was not smart enough to do a man's job.

But these problems were minor compared to the largest problem of all. Because of all the costs involved in producing an opera, the New York City Opera owed over six million dollars.

Peter suggested that Beverly close the opera house. Beverly was not about to quit.

Beverly traveled constantly, raising funds for the City Opera. She asked people to give money. These meetings were often held during meals. As a result, she earned the reputation of being the "most expensive breakfast in town." (In fact, she gained 70 pounds as a result of all the meals.) That first year, even though Beverly raised five million dollars, the company lost six and a half million dollars.

Attendance dropped at the operas. Now that Beverly was no longer singing, people just stopped coming to the City Opera. Beverly tried new ways to bring in the audiences. She brought in young and talented American singers. She offered the audiences a mixture of their favorite operas as well as new ones.

She also installed supertitles, or signs, during operas. When operas are sung in other languages, few Americans can understand what is happening. But with supertitles, the English words are flashed above the stage. Audiences quickly read the words. As a result, they enjoy the opera better, and are more likely to come back.

In the past, the City Opera had a fall and spring season. Beverly changed to a summer-fall season for two reasons. One, tourists vacationed in the summer and she hoped they would attend the opera. Two, she saved thousands of dollars in storing and transportation. Each time the opera season closed, all the costumes and stage sets had to be trucked to a warehouse in New Jersey.

These improvements did not come easily. Over the course of the next five years, major setbacks occurred. Beverly fired the office staff and then hired workers who were loyal to her. To pay the bills, she refused raises to everyone in the entire opera company. In 1983, the orchestra went on strike. The union leader accused Beverly of stealing money from the City Opera. And on Labor Day, 1985, their New Jersey warehouse burned down. All of the costumes for 75 productions were destroyed.

Sir Rudolph Bing told *The Washington Post* that "Miss Sills has so far not shown any success in her job."

In spite of everything, Beverly worked harder. In 1986, six years after Beverly was named General Director, the New York City Opera had enough money.

Attendance at the operas was increasing. Then and only then did Beverly begin looking for her replacement.

At last, in December 1988, Beverly Sills retired as General Director of the City Opera. Eight years was long enough, she said. Thanks to Beverly's hard work, the City Opera had no debts. She even managed to save more than three million dollars for the City Opera.

So what will Beverly do now that she has retired? "I've always tried to go a step past wherever people expected me to end up," she said.

Brava, Beverly Sills! Brava!

ABOUT THIS BOOK

I first heard Beverly Sills in 1978 when *The Merry Widow* was performed live for public television. As I mentioned in Chapter 6 this was one of the first televised operas. At that time, there were no VCRs, so my husband and I taped the music. We listened to it over and over again. Sometimes, we twirled and hopped and skipped around the living room floor.

In the spring of 1979, Beverly Sills came to Fort Worth, Texas, to sing in *The Barber of Seville*. My mother and I sat in the middle of the third row. My husband was on a business trip, and has always regretted he didn't see Beverly.

When Beverly sang, she seemed to glow with an inner light. I wanted to laugh and cry at the same time. One of her fans used to wear a button that said, "Beverly Sills is a good high." I knew what she meant.

To write this book, I read nearly twenty articles about Beverly and also her two autobiographies: *Bubbles* and *Beverly*. You can get an idea of her greatness, if you listen to one of her recordings.

M.K.